MARTZE

MARTZE

JACK SENDAK

Pictures by
MITCHELL MILLER

Farrar, Straus & Giroux

An Ariel Book

New York

To Martin, Laura—and Charlotte

MARTZE

Martze longed to see the sun. The rain had been falling for five days, with five more days of it a certainty. That night Martze leaned out of his window and did a magical thing. He peered into the storm, the rain blowing in his face, and he cried out, "This all must stop. Enough."

In a few moments the storm calmed down, the sheets of rain became a trickle. The moon and the stars, milky white, emerged and were reflected in the great puddles of rain water in the streets below.

Martze was stunned. Had he the power to do magic? He was shaken, and frightened.

What things he might do!

A week later he tried it again. He was lying in a field of grass, looking up at the setting sun—red, like a pomegranate.

His heart beat quickly at the beauty of it. He felt a power surging inside him. It was his magic. "I want to see something . . . a vision . . . something extraordinary," he said aloud.

Suddenly, off in the distance, he saw a girl walking on a rope stretched between two huge trees. A little bird flew next to her shoulder. The great pomegranate sun was just behind her and it bathed her in a flaming light. Martze ran towards the trees, but when he got there the rope, the girl, the bird, and the sun were gone. Had

he imagined this vision? No. No. He was certain it had been real.

Martze was sure of his magic now. He delighted in his new-found power. He could do anything. He was a magician—not in the usual sense of the word, a trickster. No, he was a boy who could do real magic. Magic. Magic. He loved the very sound of the word.

His powers were not a secret for long. He fell into a boastful mood and had to tell some of his friends. They laughed at him and called him a fool. Soon the whole village was laughing at him. "Magic boy . . . what nonsense!"

Martze was shocked by their attitude. He had never

liked the people of his village much, now he hated them. One day his friends stopped him and demanded that he show them some magic. Martze was furious. They had to see proof, did they? He would show them. He raised his arms in a mysterious gesture and shouted that they should all turn to stone. The boys fell back in fear, but when nothing happened they all burst into laughter and called him a fool.

Martze was crushed. Why hadn't his magic worked? What had gone wrong? It must be these so-called friends of his, he thought. How could he do magic when everyone considered him a fool? He would have to go somewhere else, to a village where the people were more

sympathetic and friendly. There he could do his magic. So, bidding a sad farewell to his parents, he set off down the road.

The first village Martze came to was the prettiest place he had ever seen. Each house was painted a different color. Oranges and pinks and greens and blues and violets. The walks were yellow, and there were many trees and flowers about. The townspeople, arrayed in brilliant clothes, smiled and nodded to each other as they strolled down the streets. This might be the very place he was looking for. He came to a pretty garden. On the gate was printed: *Garonce Bids You Welcome.*

It looked so inviting that Martze went in.

There stood Garonce, the fiercest, meanest-looking dog he had ever seen. The beast charged and Martze fled, escaping the flashing teeth just in time. As he ran down the street he saw an old lady beckoning him to enter her house. With the dog behind him, Martze had no choice. He dashed in. The old lady put a knife in his hand and told him to cut her birthday cake. Martze, puzzled, uneasy, not understanding anything, was about to comply when the door burst open and in came a horde of sniveling, snorting, snapping children. "We want cake too, we want cake," they shouted. They climbed onto the table and chairs, and they hung from

the walls and sprawled all over the floor. They screamed and shouted and stamped their feet. "We want cake."

Martze did the best he could. With two children clinging to his arms, he tried to cut the cake. But it was as hard as cement. He could only chip little pieces from it, which the children gobbled up immediately. "This is disgusting," cried Martze, and he ran off, the knife still in his hand.

"We want cake," shouted the children, in pursuit. And the old lady, running too, screeched, "Thief, he stole my knife." Soon the entire village joined the chase, with Garonce in the lead.

"Now is the time for magic," thought Martze. He

turned to face them, his arms outstretched. Everyone stopped in surprise. He called out in a loud voice, "Begone. Vanish. Disappear."

They did nothing of the kind.

The chase started again. Martze was heartbroken. Again his magic had not worked.

As he turned a corner he saw a pretty, dimpled little girl. She pointed to a house. Certainly he could trust her. He raced inside, only to find three policemen waiting to capture him. He flung himself out of the window and ran, stopping only long enough to give the dimpled little girl a good smack for being so deceitful. The people here were worse than his own villagers. Beneath their

pretty paint and their smiling faces, they were mean and ugly.

He leaped over a stone fence and entered a forest. It was misty and damp. He heard something thrashing about. It sounded like an enormous animal. He followed the noise until he came to the mouth of a cave. And he saw, sitting in the darkness, bent over double, his hands tied to his ankles, a huge giant. Martze was dumfounded.

"Who has done this thing to you?" he asked. The giant was silent for a while, then he explained, through parched lips, that he was the prisoner of the people of the painted village. "Why? Why?" demanded Martze.

The giant looked down at him. He had great blue eyes and he spoke in a droning kind of a voice. He said that the villagers feared him because he was so big. Martze was furious. Such villainy. Smiles hiding their evil hearts. "I will free you."

The giant groaned. "Oh woe. It is not necessary."

"Not necessary? Not necessary? You *must* be released. And such wickedness has to be punished." With the knife, Martze cut the ropes. The giant watched him with unbelieving eyes. He was free. Martze pointed towards the village. He said, "Go there and destroy it. Let nothing remain." And handing him the knife, Martze ran down a path that soon led to a good road.

The next village he came to was a strange one—and mysterious. The houses were built right next to each other, not a whisper of a space between them. They were all oddly shaped, twisted and crooked. There was just one street, and it was barely wide enough to squeeze through.

The village was deserted. All Martze could hear was the whistling of the wind. He walked down the street. He could feel eyes all about him, staring at him. Was it his imagination? "Hello. Hello," he shouted. There was no answer. Only the sound of the wind.

Then he saw a face looking out of a window. It did not move. The eyes were opened wide. Now he could see faces at every window, all staring at him with wide-open eyes. "Hello. Hello," said Martze. But they did not answer.

Martze came close to one of the windows and looked at the face. It was not real at all. The face was made of cardboard, with painted, wide-open eyes.

The houses too were made of cardboard. Pins were stuck in them to keep them together. Martze did not know what to think. Who had built this awful place? He was beginning to grow frightened now. Only the thought that his magic could save him from trouble kept him going.

At last he came to the end of the street, and there

stood a house bigger than the rest. From it came the sound of laughter. He stood there for a long time wondering whether to go in or not. It was a funny kind of laugh. "Heh heh. Heh heh." He looked back down the street, at the strange houses. Where had they all come from?

He went into this house.

A huge chair stood in the middle of the room. It was covered with velvet and ribbons, and had a pillow with a dragon painted on it. The strange laughter was echoing off the walls. At first Martze could not tell where it came from. But then, to his great shock, he saw in one of the corners a thin little man, dancing on tiptoe. He wore a crown and a long robe, which he had drawn up over his knees so that he could dance better. When the apparition saw Martze, he dropped his robes and fled to the chair, where he sat down and tried to compose himself.

After a few moments he said, "I am the king here and I want to know why you are sneaking around here like a snake."

"I am not sneaking," replied Martze hotly. "I just happened to come by your village. It is such a—an unusual place. I wanted to know more about it."

The king beamed. "I made it."

"What?"

"I built it all myself, heh heh, heh. I even made the people."

"But they are only cardboard."

"All the better. They respect me. They obey me. They love me. I am their king. Heh heh, heh."

"But—"

"And when I parade up and down the street, they watch me and cheer me."

"Still, wouldn't it be better if they were real?"

"No. No. There is no one here to laugh at me."

No one to laugh at you. Martze liked that. "Could I live in this village?"

The king looked doubtful. "I admit I do need a guard

—to keep people from sneaking around like snakes, heh heh. But you are too little. I need a strong man."

"But I can do magic. I could protect you."

"Magic?" He scratched his chin. "I guess you could pretend you do magic. That would scare off my enemies."

"Pretend? I really can do magic. I can change all these cardboard people into real ones."

"That wouldn't be wise."

"I could do it. Right now if you wanted me to."

"Look. I will make you a duke if you will pretend to be a magician. When my enemies hear of you, they will all run away."

"But I tell you—I *am* a magician."

"All right then. A prince. All you have to do is pretend you are a magician and I will make you a prince, heh heh, heh. What do you think of that?"

"But why should I pretend to be a magician when I really am one," shouted Martze very loudly. "I'd rather pretend to be a prince."

The king clapped his hand to his forehead, nearly dislodging his crown. "You *must* do as I say," he wailed.

Martze felt dizzy. The room was stifling. He couldn't breathe.

He wanted very much to leave.

Then the king said, smiling sweetly, "Hark. I hear

monsters outside, slithering down the street. Here, take this sword and bring back their heads."

Martze took the sword, it was made of cardboard. He went outside, relieved to be free of that madman. He looked all about. There were no monsters.

Should he really stay on here? The king might be right. Perhaps the best kind of people were cardboard ones. No one to call you a fool. Here he could do all the magic he wanted to.

Why not try some right now? The king wanted monsters' heads. He would get one for him.

He stretched out his arms and shouted, "I want a terrible monster, here—at my side."

No monster appeared. Martze tried again. Nothing. Nothing.

Again his magic hadn't worked, but this time he wasn't too surprised. How could his magic, which was real, work in this nightmarish place? Nothing real could exist here. Everything was fake, cardboard.

He would have to go elsewhere to make his magic work again.

He flung the sword against one of the houses. Down went the house. Martze burst into laughter. "What a foolish place this is."

He ran to another building and pulled out the pins. Down it went, knocking down another house in turn,

and another, and another. The whole village began to
topple slowly to the ground.

Martze thought it would be wise to leave now, which
he did as speedily as possible.

Martze slept under a tree that night. When he woke
up he found three men, all with long beards and armed
with rifles, looking down at him.

Martze stood up. They wanted to know what he was
doing there.

"I got lost in the woods," said Martze.

Was he an orphan?

"No, no," said Martze. "I am looking for a place to

live. I am looking for a village where I can practice my magic."

The eyes of the three men lit up. He was a magician? They could certainly use a magician in their village. Too bad he couldn't come with them, though. Only men with beards could live in their village. Boys weren't allowed there. Too bad.

The three men walked away. In a moment they came dashing back. They had come up with an idea. Why not disguise the boy as one of them? A great idea. Each of the men cut off a piece of his beard, and they tied the pieces together and stuck the new beard on Martze's chin with some sap they took from a flower.

Now he could come and live with them.

"But won't the rest of the villagers know my beard isn't real?"

The men said it did not matter. The villagers would be so happy to have a wizard living among them, no questions would be asked. They hurried him off to the village.

Getting there was difficult because the village was built along the side of a mountain. It was a long climb. Martze could not understand why anyone would want to put a village in such an awkward position, but there it was. The houses leaned perilously over the side, as did everything else. Even walking was dangerous. Martze imagined that many a poor soul went skidding down the mountainside in the dark of night.

The three men led him into the village, announcing to everyone that the greatest wizard of them all had come to live with them. The villagers went wild with excitement. They crowded around him. They hugged him. They kissed him. They threw flowers at him. They cheered him. They wept with pleasure. "Our wizard!" they cried.

Martze was overwhelmed. At last he had found a home. Here he would do all the magic he wanted to, for people who really appreciated him.

He must see their village, they said. All of it. Now.

It was the finest place in the whole world. They would not take no for an answer.

Martze laughingly agreed.

To get from one part of the village to another, it was necessary to climb, up or down. At some points the path was so steep that Martze had to hold on to somebody's hand for dear life. Up and down he scrambled, followed by the proud villagers, touring the dilapidated, weather-beaten ruins they called their homes. "Our wizard, our wizard," roared the delighted villagers. Every bone in his body ached. And when he would ask, "Is that all? Have I seen everything?" they would answer, "No, our wizard, there is more."

And off they would go, scaling the mountainside
again. Would he get through this day alive?

Once, when they passed a large grim-looking building
with tiny windows, Martze wondered if they could go
in and rest awhile. The bearded villagers said, "No, our
wizard, it is too dirty in there, there is nothing to see
inside." Martze went on, exhausted.

He even had to jump over a huge crevice. Had he
slipped, he would have fallen a thousand miles to no-
where.

At last they led him to the house where he was to
live. It was a tall stone tower, crazily perched near the
top of the mountain. Martze had to climb a hundred

steps to get to the top, and there he fell breathless on his bed.

In the morning, he looked down from his tower. He could see abundant forests everywhere. From one side, though, he saw only mist, nothing else. The forest seemed to stop abruptly there, as though the world ended at that very spot.

Martze now became aware that the tower was weaving back and forth in the wind. He hastily ran down the hundred steps.

At the door he was immediately surrounded by the jubilant villagers. They were so friendly towards him, they adored him so, that Martze felt he must thank them by finally doing some magic. He raised his arms and cried, "I will make a storm, with thunder and lightning. And I will crown this village with a rainbow."

All the villagers looked up. The sky was brilliantly clear. They stared with straining eyes. Nothing happened. But then Martze heard some of them saying that the sky did seem to be getting a bit darker. There did seem to be a little cloud out there—somewhere. They could almost see it now. No doubt there would be a storm in a day or two.

The villagers cheered him mightily. "Our wizard. Our wizard." They led him into the great dining hall, where they all sat down and ate for hours. They stuffed him with so much food and wine that Martze became miserably sick and was sure he would die.

They even made him smoke cigars and promised him there would be an even greater celebration tomorrow. Martze groaned.

Later, when more refreshments were being ordered, Martze managed to slip out. He ran towards the tower, but when he got there it was swaying so much he didn't dare go into it. He could hear the villagers shouting in the distance: "Our wizard. Our wizard." He decided to keep on running and raced off in the direction of the spot where it seemed the world came to an end.

Even though the people loved him, he had to leave

them. Celebrations. Crevices. Wine. Cigars. He was just a boy. He was only disguised as a grown-up. And besides, his magic did not work here either.

He heard a terrible crash behind him. He knew the tower had fallen.

As Martze walked, the trees began to disappear. The earth turned to sand and soon he found himself on a beach, looking at the first ocean he had ever seen. The vastness of it, the emptiness of it, the beauty of it thrilled him and chilled him. He sat down and looked at it for a long time. His eyes never tired of the spectacle. He drew deep breaths of the sharp air, which was mixed with salt and mist. After a while he took off his shoes and walked along the water's edge. The water was very cold, but he did not mind it too much.

He was lost now, really lost. Where was he to go? This was the place he had seen from the tower. It looked now as it did then, like the end of the world. He felt tired, and lonely, and bitterly disappointed.

"Oh woe, woe," he heard someone say.

Lying on the rocks, amid the angry spray of the waves, was the giant. When he saw the bearded Martze, he sat up and said, "I am looking for a little boy. If you see him, send him to me. I want him to see how sad I am." A huge tear squirted out of his eye.

"Once I was bound and left in a cave. The villagers were afraid of me, so they fed me every day. I hadn't a care in the world. Then this boy came along and cut me free. I ran to the village and told the people there I would be good and not harm them. And what did they do? They chased me away with sticks and stones.

"I have been wandering ever since, alone and hungry. I was better off in the cave. I wish I was there now."

Martze only half-listened to the story. He was watching a sea gull floating silently in the sky.

Then he heard a sound behind him. He turned and saw the bedraggled king. His clothes were torn, one shoe was missing, and the top of his crown was bent.

"They are madmen, heh heh, heh. They all have beards, and they are weeping and wailing and tearing their clothes. They say their wizard was killed and they are mourning for him. They are all marching to the sea, heaven knows why. They should be here presently."

Martze looked nervously about.

"But who cares about them?" the king continued. "I have my own troubles. Would you believe it? I once had my own empire. I built it with my own hands. Then along came this boy and destroyed the whole thing. Oh, this is such a cruel world."

Despite all his failures, Martze could not give up the belief that he really could do magic. This time he must try very hard. The other times, he realized now, were only attempts to hurt or frighten people, or to show off.

"I wish I were a king again," said the king.

"You can be my king," said the giant.

The king looked at him, surprised. He hadn't noticed him before. He walked over to him and studied him carefully.

"Could you pretend you are made of cardboard?" he asked.

The giant jumped to his feet. He was immense. "I could be anything you want me to be," he said. "Would you let me live in a cave?"

"I would let you," answered the king graciously.

"Would you stare with wide-open eyes and cheer when I parade down the street?"

"I will. I will."

"Then I shall be your king," exclaimed the king. He paused, wondering, "Where shall this kingdom be? There must be no other people about. No little boys to destroy everything."

"I know where," the giant cried. "There are islands out there in the ocean. We can choose any one of them. They are full of caves."

"How are we to get there?"

"I can carry you on my shoulders," said the giant. "I will walk across the ocean."

The giant knelt down and picked up the king and put him on his shoulders. Then he stepped into the ocean, causing a gigantic wave. The little boy watched as he walked away, chattering happily to his king.

When they were out of sight, Martze took off his beard and buried it in the sand.

Martze cupped his hands over his eyes. A spot of red was coming along the shore towards him. It was red like the setting sun.

He watched and watched and soon he saw that it was a girl, walking with her arms outstretched. She was wearing a red nightgown. As she came closer, Martze saw that her eyes were closed. She was walking in her sleep.

He touched her shoulder.

"Samson? Is that you?" she whispered.

"No. It is Martze."

The girl's eyes opened wide with surprise. She stared at him, and then she dropped to her knees.

"I was dreaming," she said. "I dreamed that I was walking on a rope stretched between two trees."

An icy chill ran down Martze's spine. He looked at her. Did she look familiar? He felt very cold.

"You have been walking in your sleep," he said. "You better go home now—"

"Home? I have no home. I live in the orphanage. I suppose the only reason I was able to walk out today was because the wizard is dead."

"What?" cried Martze.

"Yes. The famous wizard who lived in our village. He was killed when his tower fell off the mountain, and everyone is mourning for him. That's why there were no guards today."

"You are kept prisoner then?"

"The villagers do not like children. They keep us locked up in a large building with tiny windows."

Martze remembered the place.

"We are only allowed to go out into the yard in back.

That was where—that was where I—" But she did not go on.

"You called me Samson," said Martze. "Who is he?"

The girl covered her face with her hands. "A tiny little bird," she murmured.

"Did he fly near your shoulder?"

She looked at him, surprised. "How did you know that?"

"I just supposed he did," said Martze. "Tell me about him."

She sat silent for a long time. Then she said, "I have lived in that orphanage all my life. It is a sad and dreary place. Nothing to do. Nothing to look at."

Martze nodded sympathetically. The girl continued.

"Years ago there came to my window, one night, a little bird. He was sweet and friendly. I fed him some breadcrumbs and he flew away. The next day he came back and after that we were great friends. He would sit on my windowsill and chirp and chirp and chirp. He would eat his food from my hand. He would fly next to my shoulder. He would sleep on my head, the silly thing.

"Sometimes he would stay away for a few days. I would miss him very much. But, oh how I envied him, soaring happily in the sky. When he came back he would be nasty and bite me. But that was only his way.

He would soon make friends again. He was my only friend. When I would see him in the morning, I would be so happy. I can't describe the feeling it gave me. I was happy. Happy.

"The years went by and it never entered my head that my little friend was getting old. I could see the signs, but I refused to think about them. He would fly awkwardly. Sometimes he did not land where he planned to. Sometimes he would lose his balance and fall off my shoulder. And when I would laugh at him for being so clumsy, he would look at me in a sad, funny way.

"Soon he would never leave my windowsill. He would just sit there, not uttering a sound. He would not eat. At

night as I lay in my bed I could hear him cry, and my heart felt as though it would break.

"He would let me hold him in my hand. Before, when he was well, he would never let me do such a thing, he would squawk and bite at me. But now my poor little bird would lie in my hand all the time.

"Then, one day, he was very ill. He lay in my hand and looked quietly at me. I scratched his head. That night—that night—my poor old friend left me. His dear little soul flew to heaven. I looked at him and my heart was breaking. Oh, my poor old friend. He had meant so much to me. He had been my only joy.

"I didn't cry," said the girl, a single tear trickling

down her cheek. "He was very old. He couldn't live forever. But can you understand how much I missed him?" Martze nodded. He almost could.

"I would look at the empty window where he used to sit and chirp. At night I would listen for his scratching. During the day I would look at the tree in our yard. He is sleeping there now, under that little tree."

Just then the sound of weeping and mourning was heard. They looked up and saw the bearded villagers walking along the water's edge. The girl jumped up.

"Oh," she cried. "If they see me they will bring me back to the orphanage. I can't go back there. I have no friend there any more. What will I do?"

Martze stood up too. If only his magic would work again! Magic. Was his magic nothing but a dream? Had it ever happened at all? Should he dare try it again?

He looked at the girl's frightened face. How could he help her? There was no way to go but over the ocean. He wasn't the giant who could walk across it. He wasn't the king who could sit on a giant's shoulder. He was Martze, who once could do magic. He took her hand.

Come with me, Pomegranate," he said.

The girl looked startled. "Pomegranate? No, my name is—"

"It doesn't matter. I'll call you Pomegranate. Hold

my hand, Pomegranate." He clasped her hand tightly.

Then, with a suddenness that took both their breaths away, they flew into the air. Hand in hand, they flew like two birds.

They flew over the heads of the astonished bearded men.

They flew over the giant as he wandered with the king through the mists of the ocean.

They flew laughing, just for the joy of it. They were very, very happy.

And Martze knew that he was a true wizard after all. He knew that with Pomegranate at his side he would do the greatest feats of magic the world had ever seen.